Contents

Blasts from the Past

You may have seen movies where archaeology seems very exciting. Of course, most archaeologists don't spend their days chasing villains, but some archaeologists may find buried treasure. In 1995, American archaeologist, Kent Weeks, discovered the **tomb** of the sons of Rameses II, a **Pharaoh** who ruled Egypt over 3,000 years ago.

Archaeology isn't really about treasure hunting. It's about learning how people lived in the past. It's just as exciting to find the well-preserved body of a prehistoric hunter as it is to discover a lost city. An ancient garbage dump can tell us more about daily life hundreds of years ago than a golden statue can.

These archaeologists are digging in ruins from the Moche culture in Peru.

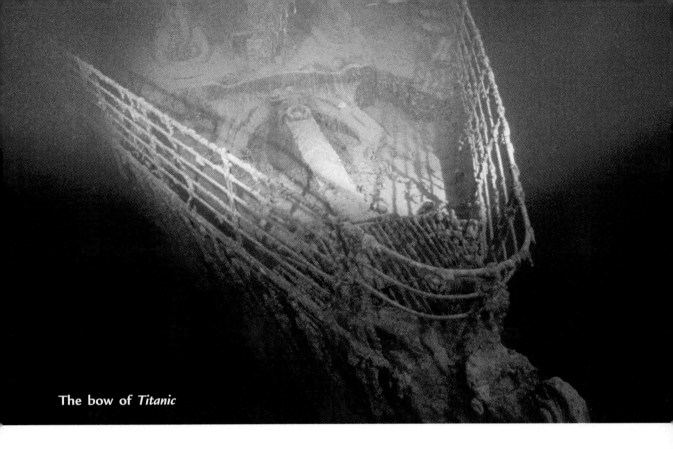

The bow of *Titanic*

What Is an Archaeologist?

An archaeologist studies the human past. He or she might dig in the ruins of an ancient city or a nineteenth-century factory.

Some archaeologists specialize in cultures that didn't build cities, such as the Australian Aborigines or Pacific Islanders. Other archaeologists search underwater for wrecked ships, such as *Titanic* or Henry VIII's ship, *Mary Rose*.

Australian Aboriginal rock painting

Some archaeologists even work with the police to uncover the truth about crimes that took place a few years ago; these archaeologists have some of the same skills as **forensic scientists**.

Why Is Archaeology So Exciting?

Archaeology is exciting because it tells us more about ourselves — who we are and where we come from. It forms a link between people from the past and people today. We learn that people from the past weren't so different from us. They laughed and cried, worked and played, worried about their families, and had arguments with their friends — just like we do.

Archaeology lets you travel back through time to ancient cities, royal tombs, and **sacred** places. So grab your hat and backpack and come along for the ride!

People from thousands of years ago even wrote graffiti; there are ancient graffiti on the pyramids of Egypt!

Otzi, the Ice-man

In 1991, two hikers in the mountains between Austria and Italy found what they thought was a murder victim. A lot of damage was done to the body before archaeologists examined it and realized that Otzi, as he was nicknamed, had died of the cold — 5,000 years ago!

SWITZERLAND AUSTRIA

Discovery Site

ITALY

Otzi was wonderfully preserved; even his eyeballs were intact. He wore warm clothes made from animal skins and carried, among other things, a beautiful copper axe.

Otzi was about 5 feet tall. He had tattoos, dark wavy hair, a beard, and a broken nose. A special sculptor reconstructed his face, as it might have looked, for *National Geographic* magazine.

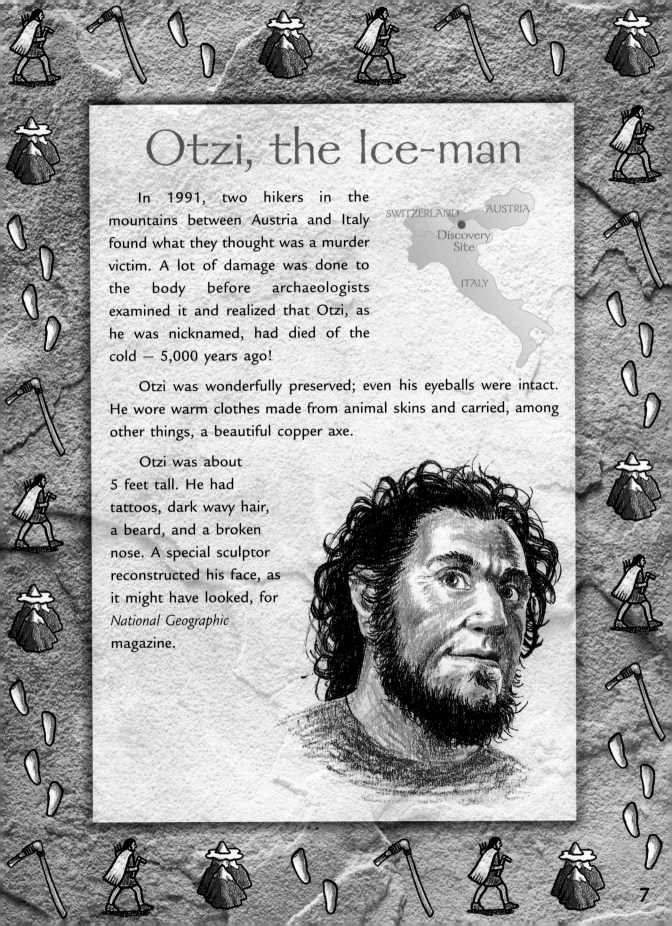

London Times

NOVEMBER 20, 1928

The Man in the Golden Mask

Discoverer: **Howard Carter**

Place: **Valley of the Kings, Luxor, Egypt**

Year of Discovery: **1922**

Years of Excavation: **1922–1927**

Cairo ○
EGYPT
Luxor ●

"I almost gave up!" says discoverer of King Tut's tomb.

An exclusive interview with Howard Carter

Howard Carter admits he nearly gave up searching for Pharaoh Tutankhamen's (Toot-ang-ka-mun) tomb.

"I'd been searching since 1919," said Carter. "By November 1922, I decided it would be my last season. Then one of my workers uncovered a step. When I arrived for work one morning, there was utter silence; they were waiting to show it to me."

Sixteen steps led down to a tomb door. But Carter didn't explore the tomb immediately.

Lord Carnarvon

Instead, he telegraphed his sponsor, Lord Carnarvon, to join him.

While waiting for Lord Carnarvon to arrive from London, the team cleared the steps to the tomb door. They also unblocked a passageway that was filled with rubble.

Finally, Lord Carnarvon arrived.

"It was the most exciting day of my life!" said Carter. "I made a small hole in a door at the end of the tomb passageway and pushed a candle through.

At first, I saw nothing. Suddenly, an amazing pile of beautiful objects sparkled before me. Lord Carnarvon asked me what I saw, and I called back, 'Wonderful things!'"

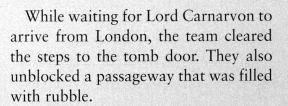

The removal of treasures from Tutankhamen's tomb, 1923

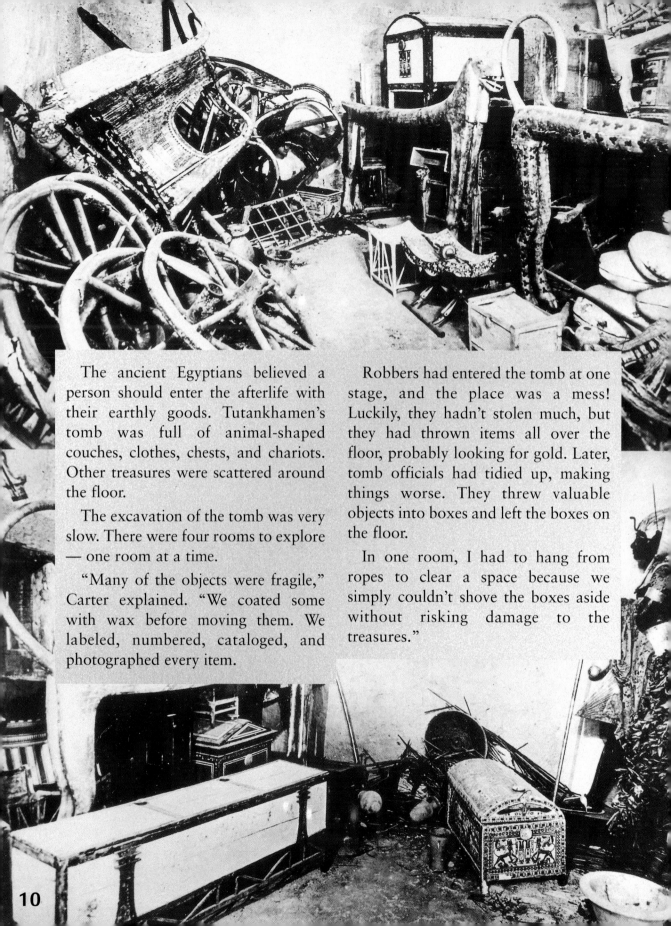

The ancient Egyptians believed a person should enter the afterlife with their earthly goods. Tutankhamen's tomb was full of animal-shaped couches, clothes, chests, and chariots. Other treasures were scattered around the floor.

The excavation of the tomb was very slow. There were four rooms to explore — one room at a time.

"Many of the objects were fragile," Carter explained. "We coated some with wax before moving them. We labeled, numbered, cataloged, and photographed every item.

Robbers had entered the tomb at one stage, and the place was a mess! Luckily, they hadn't stolen much, but they had thrown items all over the floor, probably looking for gold. Later, tomb officials had tidied up, making things worse. They threw valuable objects into boxes and left the boxes on the floor.

In one room, I had to hang from ropes to clear a space because we simply couldn't shove the boxes aside without risking damage to the treasures."

Finally, Tutankhamen's burial chamber was opened. Carter made a hole in a wall and shone a torch inside.

"I saw a gold wall! It was a huge gold shrine enclosing the king's coffin. Lord Carnarvon and I stood for a long time gazing in awe at it."

But there were problems handling the treasures.

"There were three coffins inside the shrine, each coffin inside the other. One of the coffins was made of solid gold! This gold coffin was stuck inside the second coffin. The ancient Egyptians had used an ointment as part of the burial ritual, and the ointment had simply poured from one coffin into the next, and had turned solid. We had to melt it."

The ointment covered everything except the king's head and feet. Luckily, Tutankhamen's face was protected by a wonderful gold mask and was intact."

So who was Tutankhamen?

"Tutankhamen was an ancient Egyptian king who died when he was eighteen," Carter said. "He ruled Egypt around 1341 B.C. He married Ankhesenamen (Ang-kess-en-ah-mun) when he was about seven. We know they were happy by looking at one of the tomb's paintings. Ankhesenamen is putting perfume on Tutankhamen and in another she is tying his necklace."

Is there any truth in the rumor of the Pharaoh's curse on the tomb?

"That rumor started a few years ago, when Lord Carnarvon died," Carter said, laughing. "But if anyone should be cursed, it would be me — and I'm fine!"

■

Making Mummies

The earliest known Egyptian mummy dried out accidentally in about 3500 B.C. The Egyptian climate was so hot and dry that the body was preserved in the heat and the sand. But the full mummification treatment, for wealthy Egyptians, took up to 70 days.

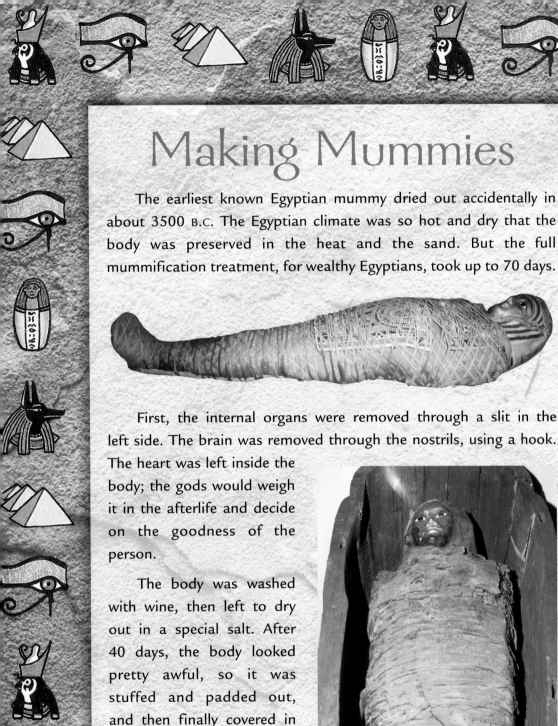

First, the internal organs were removed through a slit in the left side. The brain was removed through the nostrils, using a hook. The heart was left inside the body; the gods would weigh it in the afterlife and decide on the goodness of the person.

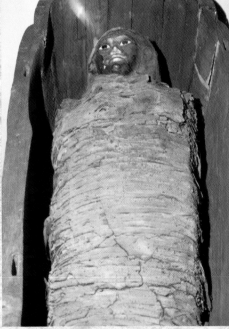

The body was washed with wine, then left to dry out in a special salt. After 40 days, the body looked pretty awful, so it was stuffed and padded out, and then finally covered in warm resin and wrapped in many yards of linen bandages.

The Treasure in the Well

Discoverer:
Edward H. Thompson
Place: Chichén Itzá, Mexico
Year of discovery: 1904

MEXICO

Chichén Itzá

Mexico City

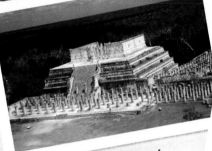

Temple at Chichén Itzá.

The sacred well at Chichén Itzá.

June 1, 1918

Dear Kathy,

Thank you for your letter. I'm thrilled to hear I inspired you to want to become an archaeologist.

I've spent 25 years of my life in archaeology. In 1885, I bought the land on which Chichén Itzá (Che-chen-et-sa) stands and lived there. I excavated the Well of Sacrifice (if you can call a lake 157 feet across a well!) and found a stone that proved the city of Chichén Itzá was built around the year 600 A.D. I battled heat, dust, giant snakes, and even spiders as big as crabs.

No, Kathy, I wasn't the first person to explore Chichén Itzá. And Chichén Itzá wasn't a lost city; it was just abandoned. A Mayan tribe called the Itzá built it. In 1841, two men (Mr. John Stephens and Mr. Frederick Catherwood) explored it. They found some wonderful **temples** and avenues, as well as a sacred well called a cenote (su-no-teh). There are no rivers in this part of Mexico, so water is precious.

Stephens and Catherwood didn't explore the cenote, so why did I?

When I was a young boy, I read a book by Diego de Landa, a sixteenth century Spanish bishop. He believed that treasures lay hidden in the sacred well. His theory was simple: people who believed in a rain-god would probably throw offerings into a sacred well. After all, it was called the Well of Sacrifice.

I couldn't stop thinking about Chichén Itzá and the sacred well. So one night, I rode to the well by moonlight. When I got there, I gazed at the water and imagined the Mayans performing ceremonies. It was then, in 1904, that I decided to find out if Diego de Landa was right. I bought a dredge, took diving lessons, and hired a trained diver to help me explore the well.

The cenote was clogged with garbage. I had almost given up searching, when I discovered lumps of incense. I was right! There was treasure in the well.

After that, we found gold, jade, jewelery, copper bells, cloth, wooden objects, and weapons. They were all preserved in resin. We also found the bones of human sacrifices.

I sent the objects to be tested in laboratories in the United States. Unfortunately, this got me into trouble with the Mexican Government, who thought I was stealing them. Eventually, I had to flee from Mexico in a boat! I don't dare try to return the objects now, so they will probably remain here in the United States.

Kathy, if you want to be an archaeologist, make sure you get some training. I didn't study archaeology, but at that time, there were a lot of amateur archaeologists. I did my best, but if I'd trained properly, I might have done less damage to the ancient objects I found. Learn as many different skills as you can — you can see how useful diving was to me! And always respect the local people, wherever you work. After all, it's their ancestors you're digging up!

Your friend,
Edward H. Thompson

Frozen Mummies

In 1995, frozen mummies from the Incan civilization were found high in the Andes Mountains of Peru. Unlike ancient Egyptian mummies, which were preserved by heat, these mummies were preserved by the cold. They had been there for over 500 years.

PERU

Andes Mountains

One mummy was found accidentally when a thaw in the snow tumbled it from its icy tomb. Even the mummy's bright, colorful clothes were preserved.

This mummy was perfectly preserved by the ice and snow.

The True Fairy Tale: Troy

Discoverers: Heinrich and Sophia Schliemann
Place: Hissarlik, Turkey
Year of Discovery: 1870

Hissarlik • Ankara
TURKEY

Excavation:
1870, 1871-73, 1878-79, 1882, 1890

Once upon a time, a beautiful Greek queen, Helen, ran away from her husband, Menelaus, with a prince named Paris. Paris took Helen to his home, a city called Troy, in what is now Turkey.

Menelaus and an army followed.

For the next ten years, the Greeks and Trojans fought a fierce war. Finally Troy was taken by trickery. Greek soldiers had hidden inside a huge wooden horse which the Trojans took into their walled city. That night, the Greek army crept out of the horse and destroyed the city of Troy.

Years later, a poet named Homer retold this story in an epic poem called *The Iliad*. The Greeks believed the story was true and that it had happened around 1184 B.C. But by the nineteenth century, most people believed it was only a fairy tale. *Until...*

Heinrich Schliemann was born in 1822 in Ankershagen, Germany. He often explored the **medieval** ruins in his area. He was a clever businessman and became a millionaire. He retired early to do something that he really wanted to do — archaeology.

Schliemann taught himself many languages and read Homer's *Iliad* in Greek. He passionately believed that the story of the Trojan War was true and decided to prove that it really did happen.

Schliemann married a beautiful, educated woman named Sophia. Sophia shared his belief in the Trojan War. A great partnership began. They began digging at Hissarlik, in Turkey.

The remains of the city of Troy were in nine layers, each layer built on top of earlier ruins. Eager to find the Troy of Paris and Helen, Schliemann dug through the layers, damaging or destroying what didn't interest him. Later, with the help of a friend, Wilhelm Dorpfeld, Schliemann learned to be more careful.

The ruins of Troy

19

Near the very bottom layer, Schliemann discovered a Troy that had been destroyed by fire. He also found a chest filled with beautiful gold objects, which he believed had belonged to King Priam, Paris' father. Not trusting his workers, he took the treasure to his hut.

A famous photo shows Sophia wearing an exquisite gold crown, earrings, and necklace, known as "the jewels of Helen."

Sophia Schliemann

But this layer was not the Troy of Homer's *Iliad*. Dorpfeld believed that Troy VI, a higher layer, was Homer's Troy. In 1932, another archaeologist decided it was yet a different layer! Digging and the debate still continues there, today.

Until his death in 1890, Schliemann continued digging at various ancient sites. Schliemann made many mistakes, but he made many more great discoveries. He has become known as "the father of archaeology."

Digging continues at Troy

What Happened to the Trojan Treasures?

It was a 45-year-old mystery that was recently solved in the 1990s. Where were the treasures that Heinrich Schliemann had taken out of Turkey?

Schliemann had donated them to a museum in Berlin, Germany, where they stayed until the end of World War II, then disappeared. For many years, no one knew where the Trojan gold had gone. The relics finally turned up in the Russian Pushkin Museum, in 1991. Russian soldiers at the end of World War II had taken them back to Russia. The treasures were put on display in 1996 and are still in Russia today. Both Germany and Turkey want them back.

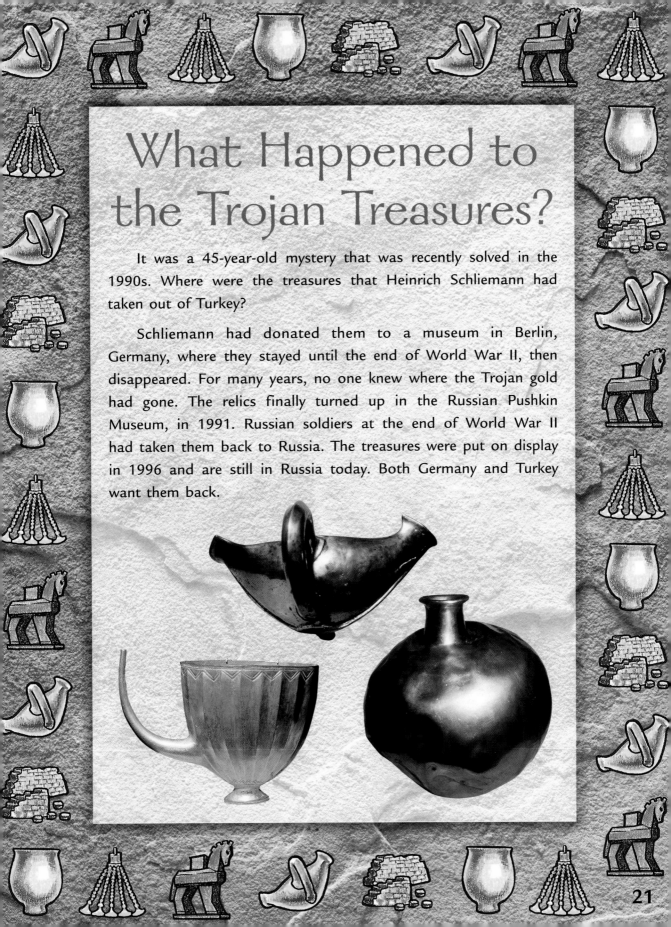

The Missing Silver Ribbon

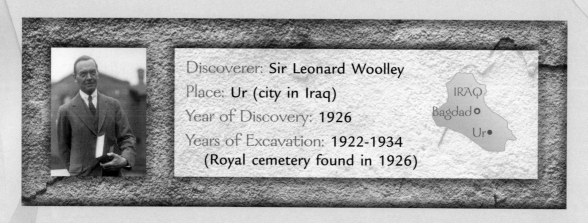

Discoverer: **Sir Leonard Woolley**
Place: **Ur (city in Iraq)**
Year of Discovery: **1926**
Years of Excavation: **1922-1934**
(Royal cemetery found in 1926)

IRAQ
Bagdad
Ur

Shub-ad hurried through the palace, straightening her skirt. She was running late.

"Where's your hair-ribbon?" exclaimed her friend, Sarai, as Shub-ad caught up with her.

"I can't find it!" Shub-ad said in dismay.

"Nevermind, then," said Sarai kindly. "Come on, quickly!"

A procession was gathering outside. There were ox carts filled with household goods and treasure, musicians, soldiers, courtiers, servants, and chariots. One ox cart at the front carried the dead king who was being taken on his last journey.

The people of Ur watched the procession march toward the cemetery. A huge pit had been dug, with a ramp going down into the earth. The procession entered the pit.

In the pit, Shub-ad and Sarai lay side-by-side with other court ladies. They felt excited; they had been chosen to accompany the king on his final journey. It was a great honor.

* * *

British archaeologist Sir Leonard Woolley found the royal court of Ur in Mesopotamia (in what is now Iraq). He even found the young lady with the missing hair ribbon.

Turn to page 24 to find out where the silver ribbon was found.

Woolley was a professional archaeologist who led a team of other archaeologists. When he found this important site early in his excavation work, he covered it up until his inexperienced team had learned their jobs.

Woolley believed that the people found in the king's grave had gone willingly. These people believed that it was a great honor to serve their king in his afterlife.

A metallic lump found in one young lady's pocket puzzled Woolley at first. All the other court ladies were wearing hair ribbons; some gold, some silver. Only this young lady didn't have one. Suddenly, Woolley realized the lump was a silver ribbon! Being silver, a chemical reaction over the centuries had turned the ribbon into a black lump.

Many objects were falling apart. One beautiful mosaic, which Woolley named the "Standard of Ur," had to be held together with wax so it could be lifted out and repaired. It was an exciting find.

The Standard of Ur

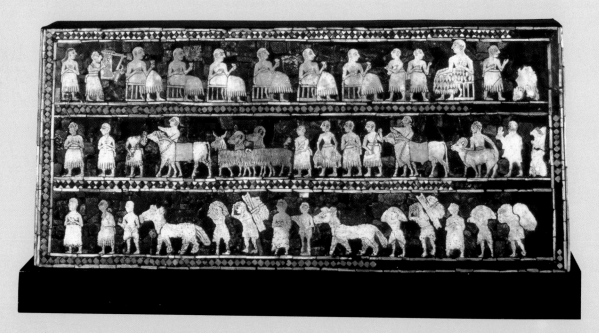

24

Ziggurats

It wasn't only the ancient Egyptians who built pyramids. There were huge, pyramid-like buildings in Central America (including Chichén Itzá) and Mesopotamia. But, unlike the Egyptian pyramids, the Mesopotamian and Central American pyramids were temples, not tombs.

The Mesopotamian pyramids were called ziggurats. The biggest, at a place called Chogha Zanbil, is 335 feet square at the base, and about 78 feet high — and this is less than half its original height!

Most ziggurats were built of dried mud brick. The outside was covered with glazed, decorated bricks, so they must have been very colorful. Often, gardens were planted on them. The famous Hanging Gardens of Babylon, one of the Seven Wonders of the Ancient World, grew on a ziggurat. It must have been wonderful to climb up through beautiful trees and shrubs to the temple at the top.

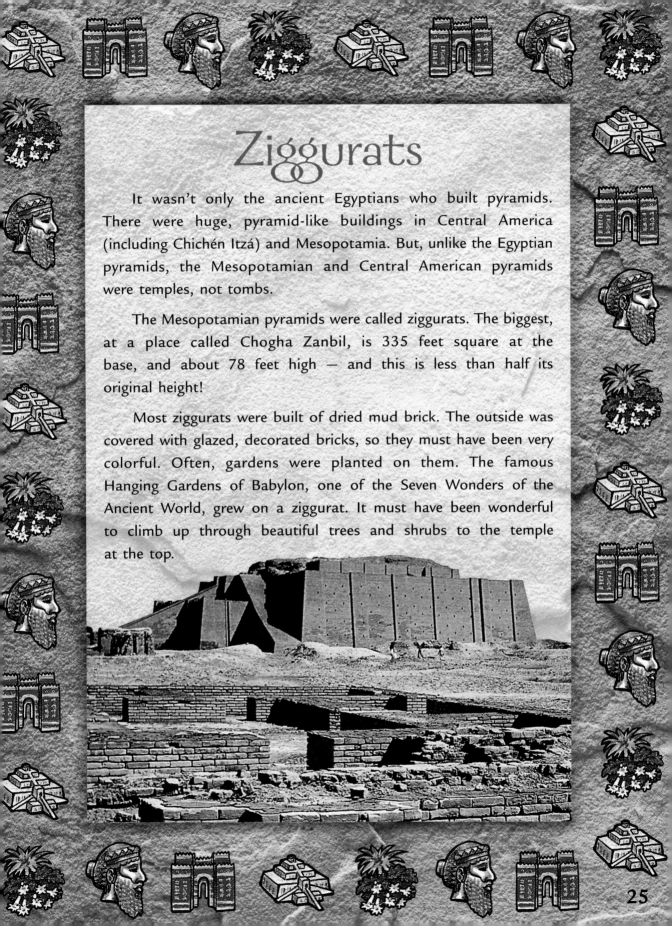

Do You Want to Be an Archaeologist?

Where Do You Begin?

Archaeology involves history, languages, geology, biology, botany, photography, and many other subjects.

Obviously, you can't study *all* of those! You'll need to rely on experts in other fields when you're leading expeditions.

Still, it's a good idea to study as many different subjects as you can.

Finding a Site

Ancient sites are found in many ways.

One way is a foot survey — that's where you walk or drive around the countryside and use special prospecting tools to locate ancient sites.

In the twentieth century, archaeology was helped by *aerial photography.* A plane flies over a promising area and spots unusual things. These unusual things might be a field in which the crops are a slightly different color from those around them, or are higher or smaller than the rest. These things suggest something might be buried underneath the crops.

An ancient find buried beneath a tell

Sometimes, ancient cities were buried under mounds known as *tells*. This happened when a city, such as Troy, kept being rebuilt on top of an earlier one.

There are also accidental finds. A developer might be starting work on a road when suddenly ancient objects or even bodies turn up.

In 1940, schoolboys at Lascaux, France, looking for a dog, found a hole and climbed through it into spectacular prehistoric caves, with wonderful wall paintings of ancient animals.

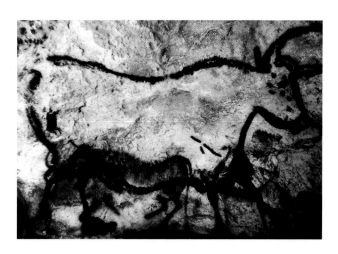

Paintings at Lascaux, France

Dating

There are several ways of finding out how old items are. This is known as *dating*.

Every living thing absorbs an **element** called *carbon* throughout its life. At death, carbon is slowly released. By testing how much carbon is left in an ancient object, such as a bone, an archaeologist can find out how old it is. Items can be dated back 60,000 years. This is called *radiocarbon dating*.

Sometimes objects are found in rock formations that contain an element called *potassium*. Like carbon, potassium changes over the centuries; it turns into *argon*, another element. Archaeologists measure how much potassium has changed into argon, and figure out how old the objects are. In Africa, ancient bones and tools were found in rocks that were dated to be nearly two million years old!

These famous archaeologists, the Leakeys, discovered prehistoric bones embedded in rocks at Olduvai Gorge, Tanzania, Africa.

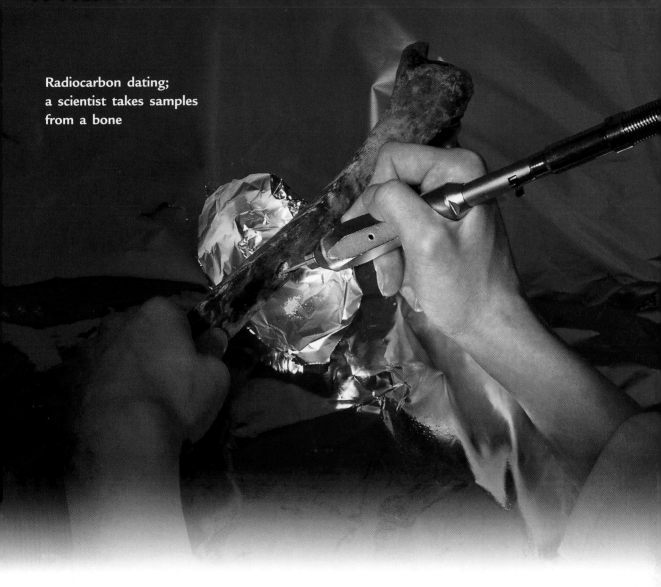

Radiocarbon dating; a scientist takes samples from a bone

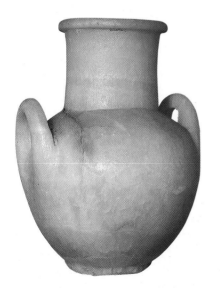

Archaeologists also compare items that are found together. In Crete, ancient Egyptian pottery was found with other objects at a site. A lot was known about Egyptian pottery and how to date it. It made sense that anything found with these pieces of ancient pottery would be about the same age.

Other Jobs

As an archaeologist, you will have to keep detailed records of everything you find. You'll also need to make maps of the site, write a report, and piece together the clues about how people lived.

You might be working on a site for many years, because you can't dig there all year round. Or you might have to work fast because developers want to build a road or a dam. This happened in Egypt in the early 1960s, where huge statues built by Rameses II had to be moved to make way for the Aswan Dam.

Statues of Rameses II were moved to make way for the Aswan Dam.

It will be quite a long time before anyone promotes you to leader of an expedition. Before that, you will have to serve your time digging, recording, labeling, and surveying the site and taking photographs.

Good luck, future archaeologist!

The Aswan Dam

Underwater Treasure

It must have been very exciting for the divers in Alexandria harbor, in 1999, when they found themselves gazing at the massive stone heads of ancient Pharaohs among the fish.

Alexandria
Cairo
EGYPT

A diver points to ancient Egyptian **hieroglyphs**

This black granite statue survived for thousands of years under the sea.

Alexandria, a city on the coast of Egypt, founded in 332 B.C. by Alexander the Great, was one of the world's great scientific and cultural centers. It had a famous library as well as the **Pharos**, a massive lighthouse, that was one of the Seven Wonders of the Ancient World. Bits of the Pharos were found along with the enormous statues.

Glossary

element a pure substance that can't be broken down into anything simpler; metals and gases are elements

forensic scientists scientists who work for the police to find out how a crime was committed; they do this by checking hairs, blood, stains, etc. in the laboratory to learn whose they are

hieroglyphs a form of writing in which pictures and symbols represent objects and ideas

medieval of the Middle Ages, a period from about 1000-1500 A.D.

Pharaoh the title of the kings of ancient Egypt

Pharos an island in the harbor of Alexandria; the lighthouse was built there and was sometimes called the Pharos or the Pharos lighthouse.

sacred very important to a god or a religion

temples buildings where a god is worshipped

tomb a building where the dead are buried